In Memory of the Magic and Artistry
of
Margot Fonteyn

Coppélia

as told by **Margot Fonteyn**

paintings by **Steve Johnson** *and* **Lou Fancher**

Gulliver Books
Harcourt Brace & Company
San Diego   New York   London
Printed in Singapore

Many years ago, in a small village in the middle of Europe, there lived a dollmaker named Dr. Coppélius. Dr. Coppélius was a true artist, and the dolls he made were even finer than those in the best shops in the great city of Nuremberg. But Dr. Coppélius, who was also something of an alchemist, dabbling in magic spells and potions, was a mystery to the other villagers.

Early one fine summer morning, Dr. Coppélius stepped out of his front door into the village square and looked up at his first-floor window. The window was thrown open and inside, apparently reading a book, sat his newest, most perfect creation, a life-size doll he called Coppélia.

She is my masterpiece, Dr. Coppélius thought to himself, *the finest work I have ever done. She looks as if she were alive.*

Dr. Coppélius smiled wistfully and went back into his house. Although he was not accustomed to the sensation of happiness and could hardly recognize it, the old man did feel a warm, pleasant glow in his heart.

Just as Dr. Coppélius disappeared into his house, the young villager Swanilda emerged from her house across the village square. Swanilda was full of the joy of one in love—she was betrothed to Franz, the most handsome and charming young man in the entire village, and she could barely keep herself from dancing instead of walking.

As she passed by Dr. Coppélius's house, Swanilda noticed the girl in the window and paused. *Surely that grumpy old recluse can't have such a beautiful daughter,* she thought. *Perhaps she is a niece come to visit.*

Swanilda stood under the window, curtsied, and smiled. "Good morning," she said.

To her surprise the girl in the window ignored her and went right on reading.

Well, they certainly don't teach manners wherever she is from, thought Swanilda. But to be pleasant she curtsied again and said, "Excuse me, I want to welcome you to our village."

Still, the girl gave no indication that she had heard Swanilda. She simply kept on reading her book.

Perhaps she thinks herself too grand to talk to mere villagers, thought Swanilda. Trying to conceal her irritation, she turned to leave, but just then she caught sight of Franz approaching. Curious to see what would happen when Franz noticed the newcomer at the window, Swanilda decided to hide close by and watch.

Franz was a cheerful fellow, and this morning he was especially happy, for he was on his way to see Swanilda. He came into the village square and was about to cross to Swanilda's house when the girl in the window caught his eye.

Doffing his hat and bowing graciously, he said, "Pardon me for interrupting you, but may I say good morning? My name is Franz."

When the young lady showed no sign of interest, Franz thought, *Perhaps being a stranger here, she is very shy.* He bowed once more. "I see you are a newcomer to our village. I bid you welcome."

Still the girl took no notice. This surprised Franz; it was the first time any young lady had not wanted to talk to him, and it stung his pride. He was just about to leave when he thought he saw the girl sway ever so slightly.

Just out of sight, the mysterious old dollmaker crouched behind Coppélia, winding up a key in her back. He was smiling, greatly pleased that Franz believed his creation to be real. In a moment the winding was done; the doll lowered her book, raised her right hand to her lips, and blew a kiss in Franz's direction.

Franz happily blew her several kisses in return. Swanilda, who had been laughing a moment before, was suddenly very jealous. Leaving her hiding place behind, she ran into the square pretending to chase after a butterfly.

When Franz saw Swanilda, he felt rather guilty. Hoping to please her, he joined the chase. With a flourish, he caught the imaginary butterfly, and taking an imaginary pin from his jacket pocket, attached it to his hat.

At that, Swanilda burst into tears. "How could you be so cruel?" she cried, and ran home.

A few hours later, the village square was full of people. The villagers were preparing for a celebration the next day, and everyone, apart from Franz and Swanilda, was in a festive mood.

At noon the Burgomaster made an announcement. "On the morrow, the new town bell is to be dedicated," he called out in a clear, crisp voice. "In honor of this event, there will be special festivities, and any couples who marry will receive handsome dowries from the lord of the manor."

The villagers were thrilled. Several young men proposed on the spot and were joyfully accepted by their sweethearts. Only Franz and Swanilda hesitated. Franz watched closely as the Burgomaster turned to Swanilda, asking if she would be wed the next day. Swanilda chose to follow the local custom of listening to an ear of wheat for her answer. If a girl should hear the wheat whisper to her, then her beloved was said to be true and she would marry him. If the wheat was silent, her beloved loved her not.

The Burgomaster held the wheat for Swanilda; she listened closely, but there was no sound. Her friends held the wheat to her ear, but still she heard nothing, not even a whisper. Even Franz tried holding the wheat, but still Swanilda heard no sound at all.

"There's no sound," Swanilda said to Franz. "You must love another."

"What do you mean?" Franz cried. But without another word, Swanilda turned and hurried away with her friends, leaving Franz alone amid the celebrating couples.

In the late afternoon the villagers left the town square for their suppers. Thankful for the quiet, Dr. Coppélius emerged from his house, carefully locked his front door with a large key—which he then wrapped in his handkerchief and tucked safely into his coat pocket—and headed to the inn for a drink. Dr. Coppélius's thoughts were on Coppélia. She was so perfect. "Ah, my beautiful Coppélia," he mused, "you are almost human. If only I could give you a real heart like mine."

Dr. Coppélius hadn't gone far, however, when he encountered a group of boisterous village boys who began to tease him.

"Come dance with us, old man," one said, laughing.

"One so lighthearted as you will surely liven our evening," said another.

Dr. Coppélius raised his walking stick and cracked one young man on the shoulder, then another on the shin. "Leave me alone!" he shouted.

Smarting from Dr. Coppélius's stick, the boys ran off. Dr. Coppélius took his handkerchief out of his pocket and wiped his brow. He was too agitated to notice that his house key had dropped to the ground. Cursing the boorish village boys, he continued on to the inn, passing Swanilda and her friends on the way.

A moment later, Swanilda noticed the key on the ground. Realizing this must be the key to Dr. Coppélius's house, she picked it up and called to her friends. "Let's try it! Let's go inside!"

The girls were doubtful.

"Come on," Swanilda urged. "I'd like to have a word with the girl who blew kisses to Franz this morning."

The girls looked at one another, then up at the shuttered house, and their curiosity overcame them. Soon they were laughing and pushing one another toward the front door.

"Shhh," Swanilda cautioned as she tried the key. It turned, and the girls slipped inside.

As they climbed the dark stairs inside Dr. Coppélius's house, the girls began to feel frightened. No villagers had ever entered the mysterious house before. What would they find?

At the top of the stairs, they reached a doorway leading to a large, cluttered room. The fading light of dusk filtered through the windows, and all about the room, in the shadows, were silent, menacing figures. They were perfectly still, even stiff, but they looked just like people.

"Are they alive?" whispered one of the girls.

Swanilda gathered her courage and entered the room. She looked closely at one of the figures, then laughed. "Why, it's only a doll!" she cried.

The girls' fear changed to delight. In a moment they discovered the clockwork mechanisms that set the dolls in motion, and one after another they wound up the doctor's wonderful creations. All around the room dolls were moving—striking drums, juggling balls, nodding, clapping—to the great amusement of Swanilda and her friends.

But where was the pretty girl Swanilda had seen in the window? While the others laughed over the mechanical dolls, Swanilda searched the dark room. At last, behind a curtain in the corner farthest from the door, Swanilda found the girl. She was sitting perfectly still with her book lying in her lap. Swanilda reached out to touch the stranger—she was as cold and lifeless as all the other dolls!

Swanilda called to her friends. How they laughed to think of Franz making such a fool of himself over a doll!

Meanwhile, having enjoyed his drink at the inn, Dr. Coppélius was making his way back home. When he reached the square and saw the door of his house wide open, terror struck him.

"Great Caractacus!" he cried. "What ruffians are destroying my treasures?" Waving his stick and shouting angrily, he ran into the house and up the stairs. "You villains," he cried. "You'll pay for this!"

When Dr. Coppélius appeared at the door, Swanilda's friends scattered and fled from the angry old man and his mysterious house, but Swanilda slipped into the corner where Coppélia sat, and let the curtain fall back, concealing her.

With the intruders gone, Dr. Coppélius sat down to recover his breath and his temper. He looked at the curtain that concealed his beloved Coppélia and saw that it was closed.

No sooner had Dr. Coppélius sighed with relief, than he heard a noise from the balcony. He jumped up and went to the window, which was being opened slowly from the outside. He stood fixed in a position like one of his dolls as Franz climbed stealthily into the room, peering about in the dim light. Then Dr. Coppélius pounced on him.

"You robber!" he shouted. "You thief!"

"No, no!" pleaded Franz. "I swear I haven't come to rob you. I saw your daughter in the window today, and I've fallen in love with her. I'd like to speak with her—with your permission, sir, of course."

To Franz's surprise, Dr. Coppélius's anger seemed to disappear and his face brightened. "You wish to speak to my Coppélia!" he said. "Then let us sit down and have some wine and talk a little."

Franz was a bit suspicious of the old man's sudden friendliness and hesitated.

"Come," Dr. Coppélius coaxed. "You have nothing to fear from me. I am just a simple dollmaker."

So Franz sat down and accepted the old man's wine. But while Franz drank from his goblet and looked around wondering where Coppélia could be, Dr. Coppélius only pretended to drink from his. Soon Franz began to feel dizzy, for the wine contained a magic potion, and in a few moments he was fast asleep.

Dr. Coppélius was overjoyed. Here was the chance to do what he had only dreamed of—to experiment with an ancient magic spell and perhaps bring his Coppélia to life.

He drew back the curtain behind which Coppélia was seated. She looked even more beautiful and delicate than he remembered.

He fetched a huge old volume and impatiently turned the pages until he came upon the spell. "Ah, yes," he muttered, "exactly as I remembered it. I must draw the life force from this sleeping youth and transfer it to my Coppélia."

Dr. Coppélius moved his hands down Franz's body from his head to his feet, all the while murmuring spells, trying to pull the spark of life from him. Then, holding what he had gathered from the boy with infinite care and gentleness, he walked over to Coppélia and showered it over her. He held his breath and waited.

To his delight and amazement, Coppélia stood up, carelessly dropped her book, and took a few steps. The old man's heart pounded; he could scarcely breathe. He returned to Franz, repeated his gestures over the boy's eyes, then once again showered the life force on Coppélia.

This time her eyelids stirred, and she blinked several times. Her arms, legs, and feet all came to life—Coppélia began to move.

Ecstatic, Dr. Coppélius returned to Franz for the third time. Trembling, he drew life from Franz's heart and transferred it to Coppélia.

"Breathe," he whispered. "Breathe."

As though touched by a caressing breeze, Coppélia's shoulders lifted and relaxed. She took a deep breath. There could be no doubt.

"It worked," whispered the old man. "I have brought her to life."

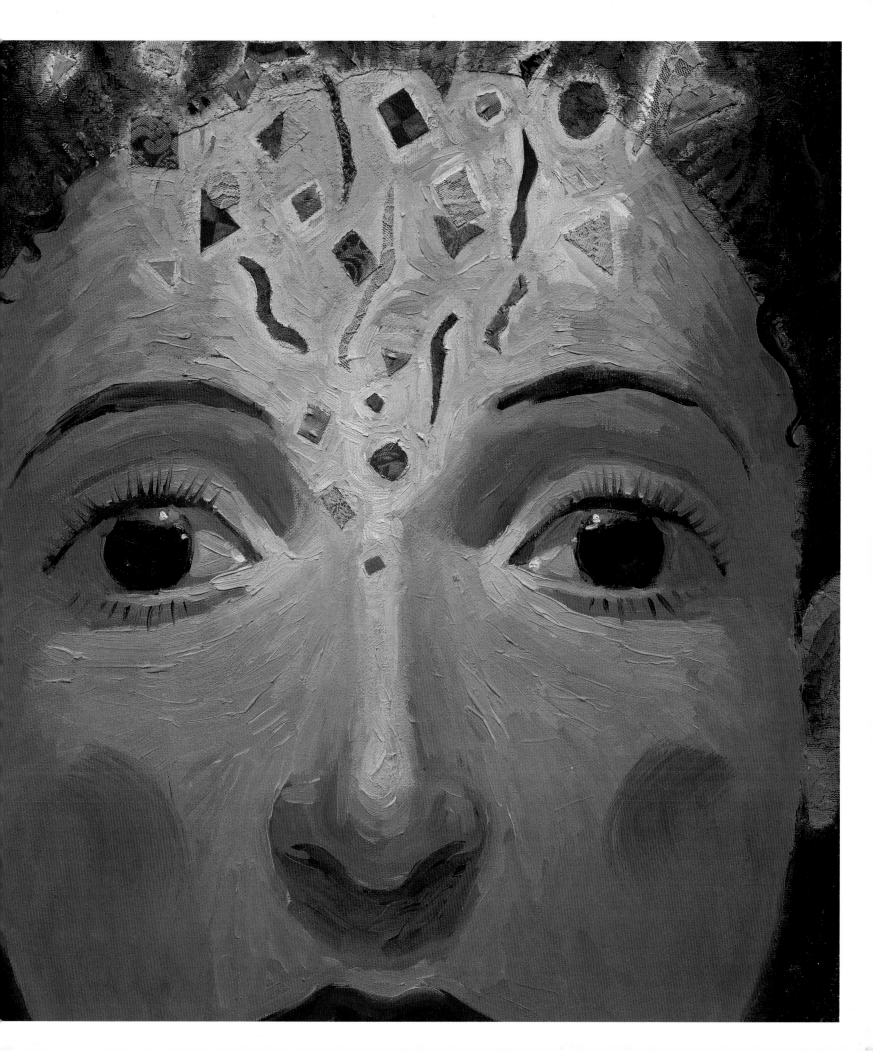

Now Coppélia, who was really the clever Swanilda in Coppélia's clothes, was waltzing about in front of the delighted Dr. Coppélius.

"Who are these people in the room with us?" she asked.

"They are not people, they are merely dolls," he replied.

"But what about this one asleep in the chair?" she asked. "Who is he?"

Dr. Coppélius assured her that he was just another doll.

"You don't mean to tell me there's no difference between these dolls and that young man?" she asked indignantly.

"None whatsoever, my dear," he said. "They are all dolls that I've made myself with love and—"

"Rubbish," she interrupted. "These may be dolls, but that one is definitely not." And she waltzed over to the sleeping Franz, reached for his wine mug, and lifted it as if to drink from it. Dr. Coppélius rushed over and snatched it from her hands.

"No, no. You mustn't," he said.

Eager to create mischief, she danced over to the magic book, reaching out to tear its pages. This was not at all what Dr. Coppélius had expected when he had dreamed of bringing Coppélia to life. Desperately, he tried to distract Coppélia first with a black mantilla and a fan, which he snatched from a Spanish doll, then with a rich tartan shawl from a Scottish doll. She danced for a moment with each, but quickly grew tired of the game and went to Franz to try to wake him.

"No, Coppélia, you mustn't," scolded Dr. Coppélius.

"Oh, mustn't I?" she retorted, and flew about the room disrupting things and setting off all the dolls' mechanisms. Dr. Coppélius did not know what to do with his unruly creation.

By this time, the effect of the drugged wine had begun to wear off, and Franz woke from his stupor. He looked about and saw at once that it was Swanilda flying about the workshop.

"Whatever are you doing in that dress?" he asked, feeling confused and also a bit guilty about his pursuit of Coppélius's daughter.

Swanilda turned to Franz. "If you want to know, come and look at the beautiful girl you are in love with."

With these words, Swanilda ran to the corner and drew back the curtain. There Franz saw the same pretty girl he had admired in the window that morning—and realized that she was no more than a wood-and-wax figure, a doll created by the old doctor.

"Oh, how foolish I have been," he murmured. "It is you I really love, Swanilda. Will you forgive me?"

Swanilda gladly did, for she was very much in love with Franz, and the two ran down the stairs to find the Burgomaster, to tell him they would indeed marry the following day.

Dr. Coppélius, left alone and stunned by all that had happened, made his way to the corner of the workshop. There he saw his greatest creation, lifeless and only partly clothed. What a fool he had been! Exhausted, and with his dreams shattered, Dr. Coppélius fell to the ground in despair.

Franz and Swanilda were married the next day with all the others amidst the great festivities in honor of the new town bell. Just after the presentation of the dowries by the lord of the manor, Dr. Coppélius appeared. He came to remind the villagers of the damages he had suffered in his workshop and to demand compensation. Swanilda, feeling sorry for the old doctor, offered him her dowry money. But the kindly lord of the manor stepped forward and gave the old dollmaker a bag of gold instead.

In the years that followed, Dr. Coppélius came to terms with his broken dreams. He realized that the satisfaction of a true artist lies in the moment of creation, not in the result, and he went on, all by himself, making more and more imaginative and perfect dolls. But he never again put one in the window of his house.

Storyteller's Note on the Ballet

Coppélia was created at the Théâtre Impérial de l'Opéra, Paris, by a French choreographer, Arthur Saint-Léon, to music by a French composer, Léo Delibes, and was first performed on May 25, 1870. A popular story called "Der Sandmann" by E. T. A. Hoffmann—a writer, critic, composer, and theater manager who had died when Saint-Léon was a year old—inspired the ballet as well as two operas and a play.

Saint-Léon had spent the 1860s as the principal dancer and ballet director of Russia's Imperial Ballet. The son of a ballet master and the husband of a famous Italian ballerina, Fanny Cerrito, Saint-Léon himself was a first-rate dancer, choreographer, and violinist. In his ballet *Le Violon de Diable,* he put all three talents to work simultaneously, accompanying himself on the violin as he danced his own choreography. Sometimes he composed the music for his ballets, and he also invented his own system of dance notation.

Saint-Léon did not consider any of the dancers at the Paris Opéra suitable to play Swanilda, but an exceptionally talented Italian girl was found in a Paris ballet school and brought in for the role. Her name was Guiseppina Bozzacchi and she was sixteen. Her dancing and personality were lively, her toe work impressed the critics, and her hands were described as unusually expressive. She was a tremendous success in the eighteen performances that were all her short life allowed her. Tragically, Prussian armies invaded France shortly after the first performance of *Coppélia*, and during the ensuing siege of Paris, Guiseppina contracted cholera. She died on her seventeenth birthday. Saint-Léon had died a few months earlier, in September 1870.

At the premiere of *Coppélia*, the part of Franz also was taken by a ballerina, the beautiful and witty Eugénie Fiocre, who was a great favorite of the male balletomanes. The balletomanes were the regular patrons of the Paris Opéra—aristocratic, rich and powerful, and not the least interested in male dancers, so it was customary for ballerinas to appear *en travestie* in the men's roles. The tradition of a female Franz in *Coppélia* was maintained at the Paris Opéra until the 1950s, though in countless versions of the ballet performed elsewhere, the role of Franz has been danced by a man.

Not surprisingly, the part of Dr. Coppélius was originally of minor importance, but it can be played for tragedy or high comedy, and performed by an outstanding dancer-actor, it can almost dominate the ballet.

This book tells in words and pictures a story that the balletgoer will see told in mime and dancing. The performers will have their own interpretations of their characters' lives and thoughts. The director may even reinterpret the whole story, but by and large, the tale of *Coppélia* will probably remain much as it is given here.

Gulliver Books is a registered trademark of Harcourt Brace & Company.

Library of Congress Cataloging-in-Publication Data
Fonteyn, Dame Margot, 1919–1991
Coppélia/as told by Margot Fonteyn;
illustrated by Steve Johnson and Lou Fancher.—1st ed.
p. cm.
"Gulliver Books."
Based on Léo Delibes's ballet after the story by E. T. A. Hoffmann.
Summary: A dollmaker cleverly schemes to pass his most beautiful doll off
as a real girl, but he is outwitted by the townspeople he tries to deceive.
ISBN 0-15-200428-9
ISBN 0-8172-5740-3 (Library binding)
[1. Fairy tales. 2. Dolls—Fiction. 3. Ballets—Stories, plots, etc.]
I. Johnson, Steve, 1960– ill. II. Fancher, Lou, ill. III. Delibes, Léo, 1836–1891. Coppélia.
IV. Hoffmann, E. T. A. (Ernst Theodor Amadeus), 1776–1822. Sandmann. V. Title.
PZ8.F668Co 1998
[E]—dc20   95-52468

First edition
A C E F D B

The illustrations in this book were done in oil, acrylic, and fabric on canvas.
The type was set in Bernhard Modern.
Color separations by Bright Arts, Ltd., Singapore
Printed and bound by Tien Wah Press, Singapore
This book was printed on totally chlorine-free Nymolla Matte Art paper.
Production supervision by Stanley Redfern
Designed by Lou Fancher